SPORTS BIOGRAPHIES

MOOKIE BETTS

KENNY ABDO

Fly!
An Imprint of Abdo Zoom
abdobooks.com

abdobooks.com

Published by Abdo Zoom, a division of ABDO, P.O. Box 398166, Minneapolis, Minnesota 55439. Copyright © 2021 by Abdo Consulting Group, Inc. International copyrights reserved in all countries. No part of this book may be reproduced in any form without written permission from the publisher. Fly!™ is a trademark and logo of Abdo Zoom.

Printed in the United States of America, North Mankato, Minnesota.
052020
092020

Photo Credits: AP Images, Alamy, Getty Images, Icon Sportswire, iStock, newscom, Shutterstock, ©Arturo Pardavila III p21 / CC BY 2.0
Production Contributors: Kenny Abdo, Jennie Forsberg, Grace Hansen
Design Contributors: Dorothy Toth, Neil Klinepier

Library of Congress Control Number: 2019956162

Publisher's Cataloging-in-Publication Data

Names: Abdo, Kenny, author.
Title: Mookie Betts / by Kenny Abdo
Description: Minneapolis, Minnesota : Abdo Zoom, 2021 | Series: Sports biographies |
    Includes online resources and index.
Identifiers: ISBN 9781098221393 (lib. bdg.) | ISBN 9781098222376 (ebook) |
    ISBN 9781098222864 (Read-to-Me ebook)
Subjects: LCSH: Betts, Mookie, 1992- (Markus Betts)--Juvenile literature. |
    Professional athletes--United States--Biography--Juvenile literature. | Baseball
    players--United States--Biography--Juvenile literature. | African American
    baseball players--Biography--Juvenile literature.
Classification: DDC 796.357092 [B]--dc23

TABLE OF CONTENTS

MOOKIE BETTS

Dominating right field, Mookie Betts is the grand slam of baseball players.

Betts is one of the most **dynamic** players in the MLB. He has won the **World Series** and many awards, including **MVP**, in his short career.

Markus Lynn Betts was born in Nashville, Tennessee, on October 7 in 1992.

His parents, Diana and Willie, chose his name so his initials would be "MLB." His mother said that as a young child, Betts would run a lot and say, "'Ball? Ball? Ball?' That's what he always wanted to do."

Betts played baseball throughout his childhood and in high school. In his senior year, he got an offer to play baseball at the University of Tennessee. However, he would never step up to bat for the school.

11

GOING PRO

Betts was **drafted** by the Boston Red Sox in the 2011 MLB draft. He made his big league **debut** in 2014. Playing against the New York Yankees, Betts made his first career hit!

Betts was chosen for the MLB **All-Star Game** in 2016. He had to have surgery on his right knee that same year.

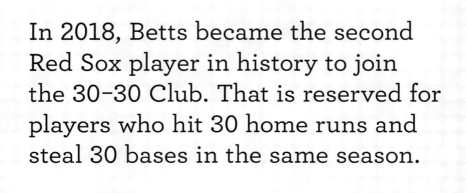

In 2018, Betts became the second Red Sox player in history to join the 30-30 Club. That is reserved for players who hit 30 home runs and steal 30 bases in the same season.

Betts and the Red Sox won the 2018 **World Series**. They beat the LA Dodgers in five games. Betts is the first player in history to win the **MVP**, World Series, Gold Glove award, and Silver Slugger award all in the same season.

17

In 2020, Betts was traded to the team he helped defeat in 2018, the Los Angeles Dodgers.

LEGACY

Not only is Betts an unmatched baseball player, he is an avid bowler. He competed in his youth at the PBA World Series of Bowling. Betts has also bowled three **perfect games**.

In his free time, Betts volunteers
with the Will to Live Foundation. The
foundation is dedicated to preventing
teen suicide. Betts also delivers food
to the homeless.

GLOSSARY

All-Star Game – yearly game played by the best players from the American League (AL) and National League (NL).

debut – a first appearance.

draft – a process in sports to assign athletes to a certain team.

dynamic – in sports, used to describe a player who can use his or her wide range of skills to do exactly what's needed at any given moment.

MVP – short for Most Valuable Player, in sports, an award given to the best-performing athlete.

perfect game – in bowling, a perfect game is when a bowler gets the highest score possible. The bowler has to make a strike in every frame to get 300 points.

World Series – a yearly series of games between the winning teams of the AL and the NL. The first team to win four games becomes the The World Series Champions of Baseball.

ONLINE RESOURCES

Booklinks
NONFICTION NETWORK
FREE! ONLINE NONFICTION RESOURCES

To learn more about
Mookie Betts, please visit
abdobooklinks.com or scan
this QR code. These links
are routinely monitored
and updated to provide the
most current information
available.

INDEX